McBROOM
and the Great Race

McBROOM
and the Great Race

SID FLEISCHMAN

Illustrated by Walter Lorraine

An Atlantic Monthly Press Book
Little, Brown and Company
BOSTON   TORONTO

Books by Sid Fleischman

Mr. Mysterious & Company
By the Great Horn Spoon!
The Ghost in the Noonday Sun
Chancy and the Grand Rascal
Longbeard the Wizard
Jingo Django
The Wooden Cat Man

The Ghost on Saturday Night
Mr. Mysterious's Secrets of Magic
McBroom Tells a Lie
Me and the Man on the Moon-eyed Horse
McBroom and the Beanstalk
Humbug Mountain
The Hey Hey Man
McBroom and the Great Race

ILLUSTRATION COPYRIGHT © 1980 BY WALTER H. LORRAINE

TEXT COPYRIGHT © 1980 BY ALBERT S. FLEISCHMAN

FIRST EDITION

Library of Congress Cataloging in Publication Data

Fleischman, Albert Sidney.
    McBroom and the great race.

    "An Atlantic Monthly Press book."
    SUMMARY: With his one-acre farm as the prize,
Josh McBroom on a giant chicken races Heck Jones on a
Wyoming jackalope.
    [1. Humorous stories] I. Lorraine, Walter H.
II. Title.
PZ7.F5992Mabd [Fic]   79–22609
ISBN 0–316–28568–4

ATLANTIC-LITTLE, BROWN BOOKS
ARE PUBLISHED BY
LITTLE, BROWN AND COMPANY
IN ASSOCIATION WITH
THE ATLANTIC MONTHLY PRESS

BP

Published simultaneously in Canada
by Little, Brown & Company (Canada) Limited

PRINTED IN THE UNITED STATES OF AMERICA

For my mother in memory

M EAN? I don't know that our neighbor, Heck
Jones, is the meanest man out here on the prairie,
but for grab-all general cussedness he'll do. Take
the time he stumbled into a patch of poison ivy. Do
you think he got the all-over itches? Mercy, no! He
gave those *weeds* a rash.

And just last July he tried to flimflam his
scrawny hens by putting pictures of chicken mash
in their feed trays. But the joke was on him! The
hens laid pictures of eggs.

That's the genuine truth, certain as my name is
Josh McBroom. I'd no more peddle fibs than I'd
pitch hay with a supper fork.

Heck Jones wouldn't rest until he'd pried us off
our wonderful one-acre farm—he'd tried many a

1

time. My, that land was rich. We could plant and harvest three-four crops a *day*. Anything would grow in that amazing topsoil, and quicker'n lickety-rip. Not long ago Little Clarinda lost her thimble, and it grew so big we use it for a rain barrel.

I'll tell you about the Great Race in a minute.

One day, toward the end of summer, Heck Jones stood on the brow of the hill. He had his hat on and a scheming look in his eye.

Suddenly, a ripsnitious wind came along and snatched him bald-headed. He ran for the hat, but his hairpiece flew someplace else. When dark fell he still hadn't found it.

"Drat!" he snapped into the wind. I was almighty surprised to learn that Heck Jones's thatch of lanky hair was a wig.

It was the next day when the young'uns discovered the lost hairpiece on a corner of our farm. By then a bird had laid an egg in it.

Mercy! Ol' Heck's wig had already grown bigger than a buzzard's nest, and the egg along with it.

"I can't wait to see what hatches out," said Little Clarinda.

"Pa, what kind of egg do you reckon it is?" asked Jill.

"Don't rightly know, my lambs," I answered. "But we owe it to Heck Jones to give him back his hairpiece."

"It'll be too big for him," Will declared.

And Chester said, "It'll cover his eyes and come down to his knees."

"Nevertheless," I replied.

Just then along came Heck Jones with the hat clamped down to his ears. He carried a barley sack.

"Howdy, neighbors," he said, friendly as you please. "And fry me brown! Look at the size of that egg! It must have taken a flock of hens all at once to lay the thing. I'll give you a nickel for it."

3

4

"Not for sale," I said. "But the nest belongs to you. I do hope you can trim it back to size. Heck Jones, that's your lost wig."

"Ain't mine," he declared, and his face turned redder'n sunset. "Now see here, McBroom, don't go spreading false rumors that I wear store-bought hair."

I shrugged. Why, the rascal was vain as a peacock! "Suit yourself," I said.

"I came out to make a trade, McBroom. Your bitty little farm for my grand one."

"No, sir," I said. "Your land is so worn out it won't grow weeds. Why, the ground is so hard prairie dogs need jackhammers to dig a tunnel."

He shut one eye and squinted with the other. "How about going into partnership with me?"

"Doing what?"

He dug into the barley sack and brought out a handful of cockleburs. "We'll plant and harvest cockleburs."

"What on earth for?"

"Leave that to me," he said, and chuckled softly.

"Not on your life. And don't drop any of those prickly seeds around here. We'd never be able to get rid of the weeds!"

"You'll be sorry," he grumbled, and turned on his heels for home.

I said to the young'uns, "Cockleburs! Imagine! Well, as long as he won't own up to that head of hair we won't disturb the nest. Let's see what hatches."

DON'T LET ME FORGET to tell you about the Great Race.

We went about our farm chores, but were careful not to disturb that huge egg. Suddenly one afternoon I heard a mighty *tap-tap-tap* from the shell.

"Will*jill*hester*chester*peter*polly*tim*tom*mary *larry*andlittle*clarinda*!" I called out. "That bird is about to hatch!"

We stood around, watching and waiting. Finally, toward dusk, the shell cracked open, and out tumbled the whoppingest big chick of a bird I ever saw.

7

"What *is* it, Pa?" asked Mary.

"An ostrich, I bet," Chester declared.

It tumbled about, trying to get the hang of its broomstick legs. "*Peep-peep-peep-peep-peep*," it began to chatter.

I scratched my chin and studied the creature from toe to head. "Nothing but a barnyard chicken," I declared. "But glory be! It is a mite oversize, isn't it?"

In the weeks that followed, the chick got its pinfeathers, and grew so tall the young'uns needed a ladder to get up and pet its back. They named her Gertrude.

Folks came from all over to see Gertrude, and feed her out of their hands. Merciful powers, how that chick could eat—and not full grown yet! She favored whole ears of dried corn, cobs and all, but she was no more particular than a goat what she ate. One time my dear wife Melissa found her trying to gobble the laundry off the line. Another time she made off with one of my shoes and gulched it down, hobnails and all. She enjoyed it so much she came looking for the other one.

Gertrude was almost full-grown when we were rattled out of bed one daybreak.

"*Cock-a-doodle-dooo!*"

I peered through the window. There was Gertrude crowing so loud she must have awakened the entire county.

"Young'uns," I said. "You got that chicken named wrong."

Gertrude was a rooster.

WHEN WINTER CAME we kept Gertrude in the barn. The young'uns had got so used to that name they didn't want to change it.

Mercy, that was a chilly winter! Doc Bumpus claimed the weather was so confounded cold his eyesight froze. But that was high summer compared to the Saturday we all gathered to put up the new schoolhouse.

I mustn't forget to tell you about the Great Race.

The lumber was cut and waiting, and everyone got busy hammering nails. The schoolhouse went up mighty fast. Didn't we sound like a flock of woodpeckers, though! The sun hardly gave out as much heat as a yellow dandelion, and the nails felt colder'n ice. But the families had brought along plenty of hot coffee and eats to share.

"Your Honor," I said to the mayor, "I never saw such a batch of dad-fangled nails. No two alike, and some as fat as carrots."

"Handmade," he explained. "Heck Jones sold 'em to us cheap. He reckoned it was his civic duty."

I was surprised that Heck Jones had taken up the nail-making trade. I'd never known him to do a lick of work. He was nowhere in sight, but I reckoned that a benefit. He was so twisty in his ways he wouldn't be able to drive a nail straight unless he got someone else to hold the hammer.

We got the school bell hung, and everybody

stood around hoorayin' and yippin' and applaudin'.

"Ain't that the prettiest schoolhouse you ever saw?" the mayor called out. "Built solid, too. It'll stand forever, and a few years more."

Just then the wind took a shift. I was hanging the thermometer, and saw the mercury drop like a shooting star.

"Head for home, neighbors!" I yelled out. "A blue norther has cut loose, and blowing this way!"

Folks began to scatter to their buggies and wagons.

"Willjillhesterchesterpeterpollytimtommarylarryandlittleclarinda!" I shouted. "You'll freeze in your tracks! Pile into the car."

I raced for our old Franklin automobile and began cranking the engine. My dear wife Melissa had snatched up Little Clarinda, and was counting noses to make sure we weren't leaving any of the young'uns behind.

"Pa!" Will said, pointing. "Look! Our shadows are lying over by the schoolhouse."

"It's no time for jokes," I said, jumping behind the wheel.

"But it's true," Jill declared.

I glanced back at the schoolyard. Merciful powers! I never saw such a sight. That sudden blast of cold had frozen everyone's shadow to the ground.

I TELL YOU, it felt mighty peculiar to walk around all winter without our shadows. But there was worse yet to come.

"Pa," Tim yelled out. "There's a bear making tracks this way."

No—it was Heck Jones hauling a bear rug.

"Howdy, neighbors," he called. "Here's a gift for you. A fine bear rug."

Just then his feet slipped out from under him. His arms shot out, his hat flew off, and he took a bone-rattling fall.

"My leg!" he wailed. "I must have busted it. Help!"

Will helped me carry him ever so gently into the parlor while the other young'uns dragged in the

16

bear rug. They set it before the fireplace, and we laid him out on all that soft, deep fur. My dear wife Melissa tucked a pillow under his head.

I sent Will and Jill to fetch Doc Bumpus. When I went outside to find Heck's hat I saw what he'd slipped on. A wolf's shadow had frozen to the ground, and it had iced over slicker'n plate glass.

Doc Bumpus turned up with his black bag and thick glasses, and began to examine the new scarecrow the young'uns had stuffed and stitched together.

"The patient is dead and deceased," he announced sadly. "No more heartbeat than a turnip."

"That's a shagrag scarecrow," I said.

"Dear me," he mumbled. "I'll be glad when spring arrives and my eyesight thaws out."

I didn't rightly believe the tale he had spread about his sight freezing in the cold, but it did come in useful to cover his mistakes.

"Heck Jones is over here," I remarked.

Doc Bumpus polished his glasses. After another examination he declared, "Broken neck."

"You're examining his leg," I said.

"Am I? Well, then, it must be a broken leg."

It took him an eternity to get a splint on, and I turned to Heck Jones.

"I'll roll you home in a wheelbarrow."

Doc Bumpus snapped his bag shut. "The patient ain't to be moved. His leg feels like it was hit by an earthquake. Be lucky to heal before spring plowing."

Oh, what a doleful look came over the young'uns' faces! But Heck Jones was smiling from ear to ear. "Another pillow, my kind Mrs. McBroom, if I could trouble you."

Heck Jones had us waiting on him foot and hand. Confound that man! The young'uns darned his socks and polished his boots. He was so fond of Melissa's drop biscuits he asked for them three times a day.

"Chester, another log on the fire," he bleated humbly. "My poor old bones are frosted over."

It was too cold for the young'uns to play outside, and they had to be mouse-quiet inside. They had hardly started a game of tiddlywinks when he sighed. "Peace and quiet, little neighbors. A sick man's got to get a full ration of sleep."

But nights he kept us all awake. Heck Jones snored so loud he rattled the windows. As the weeks dragged by we got to looking sad as bloodhounds.

"Pa," Jill whispered, "his leg must be mended by now. Can't he go home?"

"We've got to follow the doc's orders," I reminded her.

"Maybe that leg was never busted at all," Will grumbled. "Doc Bumpus doesn't know parsley from peeled onions."

"Oh, the pain," Heck cried out, as if he'd overheard us. "Polly, could you spare me your pillow to put under my leg?"

After a month of Melissa's cooking he looked fit as a jaybird. But he hardly moved off that bear rug.

"Reckon I'm doomed to spend the rest of my days a helpless invalid," he said, a tear dropping from his eye. "And to think I used to win prize money for my footracing. Nothing could catch me."

Little Clarinda piped up, "I'll bet Pa could run faster."

"Hee-haw, child," said Heck Jones, with a smirk.

But that gave the young'uns an idea. I found them out in the barn when I went to fill Gertrude's feed tray with ears of dried corn.

"Pa," Jill said. "Do you think Heck Jones would stir off that bear rug if he thought he could beat you in a footrace?"

"There'd have to be a prize," Tom declared. "I'll bet his leg would mend overnight."

I puckered my lips thoughtfully. "Might work," I said. "A splendid notion, my lambs. What kind of prize?"

"We could grow him those cockleburs if he wins," Hester put in.

I smiled. "Worth a try!"

Heck Jones had his cheeks full of drop biscuits when I fixed an eye on him. "Too bad about your busted leg, Heck Jones. I don't believe you ever ran a race in your life. There'd be a prize if you could beat me."

His eyebrows gave a flutter. "A prize? What prize?"

"Cockleburs. An acre of cockleburs."

"Well, no," he said. "I'd best do what the doc says and rest myself on this bear rug." Then a smile, thin as a crack in a cup, spread from his lips. "But I might be persuaded to go against doctor's orders if the stakes were a mite higher."

"What stakes?"

"Our farms. Yours against mine."

"No, sir," I said. "I wouldn't take your hard-scrabble farm as a gift. A sparrow couldn't scrape together enough dirt to take a dust bath."

He settled his head back on the heap of pillows. "Suit yourself, McBroom. You'd have the advantage of me, anyway, me with my leg in a splint. I'll just rest by the fire until I get my health back."

I groaned at the thought. Confound the man! It would be months before we got him out of the parlor. But I had nothing to fear in a footrace. He was so naturally crooked he wouldn't be able to run a straight mile. And lazy, too. He'd be lucky to come in last.

I shot out my hand. "A race to the new schoolhouse, Heck Jones. Agreed?"

"But that's a good five miles."

"Farm against farm."

"Agreed," he declared. He reached out his limp, spidery hand and we sealed the bargain.

I'd let him keep his farm, but we'd get him out of the parlor at last.

"We'll race tomorrow," I said.

"Hee-haw and naw-no," he snickered. "Spring thaw is soon enough. I'll need to get my strength back for a great race like that. Another platter of drop biscuits, Mrs. McBroom, if you'll be so kind."

HECK JONES busied himself scratching out a letter by the firelight. He hee-hawed in his sleep all night long. In the morning he said, "Peter, be a good lad and mail me this letter in town."

There was no shedding ourselves of that hee-hawing man! And spring was still a long way off.

"Heck Jones," I said. "The race is off."

"A handshake is a handshake, McBroom," he snorted, "and a race is a race. Soon as my leg is fit—"

Just then a monstrous growl shook the room. I saw Heck Jones go flying across the parlor as if he'd been kicked by a mule. Only it wasn't a mule. It was that bear rug.

It still had the bear in it.

25

I'll be thundered if the warm fire hadn't stirred it out of hibernation ahead of season.

Heck Jones streaked it out the door. His legs were going like a squirrel's in a cage.

And we weren't far behind him.

That gift rug climbed out through the kitchen window, but not before helping himself to Melissa's drop biscuits and a crock of honey.

Heck Jones glanced back from the brow of the hill. He'd made faster time than a quarter horse. The young'uns were right. He was fit as could be! Doc Bumpus didn't know a broken leg from cold mush.

"Hee-haw, McBroom!" Heck Jones called. "A handshake is a handshake, and a race is a race. Your farm against mine!"

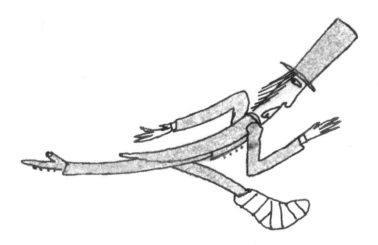

I TRIED not to let Melissa and the young'uns know that I was a mite worried about the race. It had caught me by conflabbergasted surprise to see Heck Jones so fleet of foot.

But they'd seen him too, and Will said, "Pa, hadn't you better practice for the big race?"

"Not worth the bother," I remarked with a chuckle. "I've plenty of running steam."

"Please, Pa," said Jill.

I shrugged. "Well, I reckon it wouldn't hurt to exercise my legs a bit."

I started easy, running around the farm a few times before breakfast. Before long I was trotting a mile down the road.

"Hee-haw, McBroom!" Heck Jones called out

from the brow of the hill. "I've seen house paint run faster than that!"

I grit my teeth, and kept at it. Before long I was sprinting two and three miles at a time, with the young'uns clocking me. My, I was getting quick on my legs!

I'll admit I got a bit overconfident. Toward the end of winter I carried out my hot supper plate, and a knife and fork, and set them on a corner of the farm. Then I streaked to town and back to see if I could eat my grub before it got cold. No, I never did make it, and mislaid my supper fork in the bargain.

But I did get so quick I could blow out the lamp at night, and jump into bed before the room fell dark.

Spring thaw arrived early and caught us by surprise. The sun came out hot as a blast furnace, and I wondered about our shadows left behind at the schoolyard. They'd thaw without us!

I grabbed a yardstick, called the family, and cranked up our Franklin automobile.

"Pile in and hang on!" I shouted. "Not a moment to lose!"

Folks everywhere were trying to locate their frozen shadows. My, what a helter-skelter! When we reached the schoolyard I measured the young'uns with the yardstick to make certain they got their own shadows back.

But they'd grown some, and to this day their shadows are a mite short.

Oh, how the animals got muxed up! We soon learned that a cow down the road picked up the shadow of a flock of hens. And there's many a dog in the county throwing a cat's shadow—fight something awful.

The schoolhouse began to creak in the sunshine, and some of the shingles seemed to melt off the roof. I didn't know what to make of it.

31

"Sloppy hammering," grumbled the mayor.

"Maybe it's those sloppy nails," I said.

Just then Heck Jones came by, driving a wagon. A big crate sat on the wagon bed, and it had words painted on it: PRODUCT OF WYOMING.

"Wyoming?" Peter muttered. "Pa, that letter Mr. Jones had me mail for him. It was addressed to Wyoming."

"That box has holes in it," Larry remarked. "Wonder what's inside?"

I shook my head. "No idea," I said. "But bless my suspender buttons! Look there! Heck Jones must

have been in such a hurry to collect that box he didn't bother to locate his own shadow. Isn't that a wolf's shadow he's casting?"

"A toothy one, too," said Chester.

Indeed it was. Slavering and mighty scaresome.

"Spring thaw is here, McBroom!" Heck Jones gave a shout. "Race you tomorrow!"

The mayor's ears lifted right up. "A race, do you say?"

"Stretch out a red ribbon, Your Honor," said Heck Jones. "First one of us to bust through the ribbon wins."

"And I'll be here to see that it's done fair and square," declared the judge.

The thaw didn't last long. The sun ducked behind some clouds and went out like a wet match. The mercury tumbled, and the schoolhouse stopped creaking and shedding shingles. But the day didn't turn so cuss-fired cold that our shadows froze to the ground again.

Heck Jones looked back over his shoulder. "Hee-haw, McBroom! You couldn't run a temperature and win!"

I WAS RESTLESS all night long. Heck Jones hadn't done a speck of running practice. I smelled trickery. The thought that I might come in last gave me head-to-toe shivers. But there was no way out. I'd given my handshake.

The alarm clock went off like the sound of doom, and I jumped out of bed. I ran around the farm six or eight times to limber up. Daybust broke through the tumble of clouds long enough for me to catch sight of my shadow following along the ground.

At breakfast the young'uns surprised me with a banner to pin across my back. They'd sewn silk letters on it.

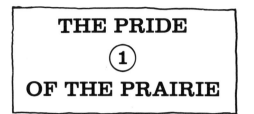

THE PRIDE
① OF THE PRAIRIE

I was almighty touched. "Thank you, my lambs. Once the race starts, Heck Jones will need a spyglass to read the fine print."

My dear wife Melissa was trying to look cheerful. But I could tell that she was dreading the race. "Nothing to worry about," I said. "When I was running around the farm just now—why, it took my shadow a whole lap to catch up with me. And I wasn't even going full throttle!"

The sky had darkened over by time the mayor turned up. He carried a gun to start the Great Race. "News has spread all over the county," he said, beaming. "Folks are lining up at the schoolhouse. The red ribbon is stretched and the judge is at the finish line to declare the winner. Let's start."

Jill and Hester pinned the banner to my back.

"I'm ready," I announced.

But Heck Jones was taking his time. The day had turned so dark it would be a wonder if we could run the race without lanterns.

"Pa!" Chester shouted. He was the first to spot Heck Jones. "And look what he's riding!"

I about jumped out of my shoes. He was mounted on a long-eared, squirrel-toothed creature with the hindquarters of a deer. The two ends didn't seem naturally to go together. I thought I was seeing things.

"Howdy, neighbors," said Heck Jones. He'd brought along the barley sack full of cockleburs. "Get out the deed to this farm, McBroom. I'll want to plant a crop as soon as I get back. What animal are you going to ride?"

"Ride!" I snapped out. "This is a footrace."

"We didn't make any such bargain. Did you think you could put one over on me, McBroom? Me, with a limpy leg?"

"There was no limp to your leg when that bear rug rose up."

He stifled a morning yawn. "Run on your own two feet, or ride. No matter to me. A race is a race, and we shook on it."

"What's that critter you're sitting on?"

Heck Jones ripped out a laugh. "Fastest animal on four legs. Half jackrabbit and the other half antelope. You're looking at a genuine Wyoming *jackalope*."

The young'uns gazed up at me, hardly taking a breath. They knew I wasn't going to be able to outrace that Wyoming mongrel.

Just then there came a mighty cockcrow from the barn, and the young'uns all tried to talk at once.

"Pa!"

"Gertrude!"

Of course! Glory be! That big rooster had running legs taller'n flagpoles.

"Your Honor, let's start the race," said Heck Jones.

"Not before I mount up," I declared.

Heck Jones shot me an uneasy glance. "Mount up what?"

The young'uns beat me to the barn, where Gertrude was gobbling up an ear of dried corn from the bin.

"Will," I said. "Fetch the ladder. And Peter, I'll need a strong rope to hang on to. Jill, get your fishing pole and tie half a dozen ears of corn to the end."

Didn't the young'uns get busy! Before long we had a kind of rope bridle around Gertrude's head and beak. I took the reins and climbed the ladder to seat myself on the chicken's back.

Jill handed me the fishing pole. Mary and Larry threw open the barn doors, and I dangled the ears of corn before the rooster's eyes.

"Come on, Gertrude. Chick-chick-chick. This way!"

And out the barn we shot.

When Heck Jones saw that bull chicken he looked as though he'd swallowed his teeth. Gertrude towered over his infernal jackalope.

The mayor was losing patience. "Is this dad-fangled race ready to begin? Folks are waiting at the schoolhouse. On your marks. Get set!"

40

41

He raised the pistol into the air and fired. "Go!"

That gunshot scared both ends of the jackalope. It jumped one way at the front and bucked another way at the rear. Heck Jones had to hang on like a tick.

Gertrude wasn't too pleased, either. His wings flapped out, knocking the mayor over, and I swear that chicken *flew* a quarter of a mile down the road. He got over his fright, and I cast the fishing pole, dangling the ears of corn in front of Gertrude's beak.

I could hear Melissa and the young'uns giving a cheer. When I looked back Heck Jones still hadn't got both ends of the jackalope to agree on one direction to run.

GERTRUDE WENT STRUTTING down the road steady as a clock. I could hear Heck Jones rant and rave, and he finally got the jackalope headed in the right direction.

Great guns, that Wyoming creature was fleet-footed! Every time I looked back it had gained on us. Its jackrabbit ears were laid back and its hind hooves rattled like dried beans poured in a pan.

"Chick-chick-chick!" I sang out.

"Skedaddle-skadoodle!" Heck Jones laughed. "Faster, you twitchy-nosed varmint!"

We hadn't gone a mile before my heart began to sink. Heck Jones had caught up. Gertrude and the jackalope were running neck and neck.

"Chick-chick-chick!"

"Hee-haw, McBroom. The farm's mine!"

"You haven't broken the ribbon yet!" I shouted back. "Gertrude, a mite faster, if you please."

Heck Jones kept jabbing his sharp heels into the jackalope, and pulled ahead.

Well, there were miles to go, and I was surprised to see that we began to gain. The product of Wyoming was running out of wind! Heck Jones ought to have had the sense to pace it.

"Skedaddle!" he ripped out angrily. "Skadoodle!"

The next thing I knew he dug a hand into the barley sack and began to scatter cockleburs in our path.

Horrors! Gertrude began lifting his feet as if he were walking on tacks. But worse! The rooster cocked his head to see if those prickly seeds might be good to eat. He slowed to stock still and pecked one up. He clucked. That ever-hungry fowl would eat anything.

"Gertrude!" I exclaimed, trying to hold his head up by the reins. But that rooster was too strong for me.

The clouds drifted away. The sun appeared, bright as summer and hot enough to melt ice. Gertrude began bobbing his head, peck, peck, peck. That overgrown rooster *liked* cockleburs.

HECK JONES was far ahead down the road. He looked back and laughed. "The Pride of the Prairie! Hee-haw!"

I grit my teeth and unpinned the banner on my back. I slipped down one of Gertrude's legs and square-knotted the banner tight around his beak. Then I tried pulling him by the reins through the minefield of cockleburs. He tried to squawk and gave such a flap of wings that the wind lifted me into the air. Glory be! The breeze also sent the cockleburs flying like birdshot. The road was clear!

I shimmied back up Gertrude's leg, and gave the reins a shake.

"Chick-chick-chick!"

I dangled the ears of corn, and the rooster went

high-stepping down the road. I declare if Heck Jones hadn't done us a favor. Gertrude had had a chance to catch his breath! He strutted along like greased lightning.

The scenery whizzed by. But Heck Jones was still a mile ahead, and I could see the schoolhouse standing in the sun. Folks were lined up along the road at the finish line. As I drew closer some of them began waving their hats.

"Come on, McBroom!"

Gertrude was gaining ground, but I was still looking at the venison end of that jackalope. Heck Jones's heels were jabbing so deep into the creature's ribs they almost clicked together.

I could see the red ribbon clearly now. It was stretched across two posts in front of the school-house.

Folks were yelling themselves hoarse.

"Step on it, chicken!"

"Heck's almost at the finish line!"

I could see that for myself! And there stood the judge ready to declare the winner.

I do believe tears sprang into my eyes. Heck Jones hardly had another twenty feet to cover.

"Skedaddle, skadoodle, skadiddle!" Heck Jones ripped out victoriously.

I patted Gertrude's neck. "Easy. No point in wearing yourself to a frazzle, my pet. You did your best and then some. Heck Jones has beat us to the finish line."

What happened next caught me by enormous surprise! That jackalope saw the red ribbon in its path. It didn't break through. It *jumped* the ribbon.

And Heck Jones was bucked off into the school-yard.

"The winner!" the judge shouted.

"Not yet!" I called out. "First one to *break* the ribbon!"

"I stand corrected," the judge declared. "The race is still on."

But mercy! I'd been too busy to notice that the banner had slipped off the rooster's beak. And in the last minute excitement I'd forgot to concentrate on the fishing pole.

Gertrude caught an ear of corn and stopped in his tracks to eat.

We stood not twelve feet from the ribbon.

"Chick-chick-chick!" I cried out. "Only another step or two!"

I tugged on the fishing pole, but the rooster had a firm purchase on the feast he'd been chasing.

Everyone began to yell, and the men slapped their hats.

"Giddyup, rooster!"

"Come on, McBroom!"

But Gertrude wouldn't budge.

Meanwhile, Heck Jones was footing it back to the jackalope. Only he'd forgot that the sun was out. He'd forgot his wolf's shadow.

He'd hardly caught up the reins when the jackalope saw that toothy, slavering shadow. The creature all but jumped out of its hide. Its hindquarters gave a mighty kick, and Heck Jones went

flying across the yard and crashed through a schoolhouse window.

"Chick-chick-chick," I urged. "Be so kind as to take another step or two!"

But Gertrude wouldn't lift a foot.

Heck Jones emerged from the schoolhouse, madder'n the devil without a match. He bent low and tried to sneak up on the jackalope.

I slipped down Gertrude's neck and tried to tug him across the finish line. It would have been easier to pull a hog through a knothole.

Suddenly I felt a smile spread over my face, and

I muttered. "That was a good race, Gertrude. My dear wife Melissa thanks you. Willjillhesterchesterpeterpollytimtommarylarryandlittleclarinda thank you. And I thank you."

I dropped the reins. I waved to the crowd and *walked* across the finish line, breaking the ribbon.

"The winner!" the judge called out.

It was just then that the mayor drove up with Melissa and the young'uns. There was a mighty roar from the crowd.

And the schoolhouse collapsed like all its nails had been pulled at once. The timber fell with such a sudden roar that the jackalope was seized by a fresh panic, and lit out in the general direction of Wyoming.

Heck Jones was all but buried in the timber, and the schoolhouse bell fell on his head.

"What in tarnation happened!" the mayor growled in a rage. "Who stole all the nails?"

The judge picked up one of the boards and studied it. "The nail holes are dripping wet. The nails melted in this spring thaw."

"Impossible!" answered the mayor.

"It's my considered judgment," declared the judge, "that we were sold assorted icicles painted silver to look like nails."

53

The mayor's face turned so hot it began to melt the starch in his collar. "Heck Jones! We'll run you out of town!"

"My patient can't be moved," announced Doc Bumpus, who was at Heck Jones's side in the pile of lumber. "The man is suffering from a compound ringing in the ears. His head sounds like a bell!"

AFTER THAT, Heck Jones kept himself hard to find.

By the time spring weeds were up we got the schoolhouse hammered back together—with real nails. On our wonderful one-acre farm we were kept busy grubbing out heaps of cocklebur weeds. Heck Jones had been infernally careless, drat his hide.

But I did hoe up the supper fork I'd lost when I was practicing footracing. I was in the barn one day, fork in hand, when there stood Heck Jones.

"You won the race fair and square," he said. "And I'd like to make amends for those school-house nails."

Why, he's a changed man, I told myself. Getting struck by the schoolhouse bell must have done his head some good.

56

"Splendid, neighbor," I remarked.

"I could raise a heap of money, McBroom, if you'd let me have that crop of cockleburs. You'll be glad to be rid of them."

"Indeed I would," I answered. "But cockleburs wouldn't bring you a nickel a ton."

"Oh, yes they would!" he said, a sudden gleam in his eye. "I figure to sell 'em to city folks as porcupine eggs."

I ran the rascal off with my supper fork. He looked back only once, as if the devil were chasing him. In our amazing topsoil that supper fork had grown into a pitchfork.

Then I returned to the barn, and pitched some more hay.